Disney

3-Minute

Bedtime Stories

pi kids® publications international, ltd.

Published by
Louis Weber, C.E.O., Publications International, Ltd.
7373 North Cicero Avenue, Lincolnwood, Illinois 60712

Ground Floor, 59 Gloucester Place, London W1U 8JJ

Customer Service: 1-800-595-8484 or customer_service@pilbooks.com

www.pilbooks.com

p i kids is a registered trademark of Publications International, Ltd.

Manufactured in China.

ISBN-13: 978-0-7853-9735-9
ISBN-10: 0-7853-9735-3

8 7 6 5 4 3 2 1

CONTENTS

Bambi

Adapted by Kate Hannigan
Illustrated by the Disney Storybook Artists

Deep in the woods on a bright spring morning, a young rabbit called Thumper ran to Friend Owl's tree with some exciting news. The new Prince of the Forest had just been born!

The animals gathered around the tiny deer and his mother. She told them his name was Bambi and soon introduced him to all the creatures of the woods. Bambi met Mrs. Quail and her chicks, Mrs. Opossum and her babies, and even Mr. Mole, who lived underground.

Bambi also made friends with Thumper. The rabbit laughed when Bambi stumbled on his long legs. He said Bambi didn't walk very well. "What did your father tell you this morning?" asked Mrs. Rabbit. Thumper knew he was in trouble. "If you can't say something nice," Thumper said guiltily, "don't say nothin' at all."

Bambi laughed and played with Thumper and his rabbit brothers and sisters. They taught the young deer the names of all the new things he discovered in the woods. Bambi saw birds and butterflies and flowers. He even met a friendly skunk and called him Flower, too.

Bambi

One sunny afternoon, Bambi's mother walked him through the forest to the open fields of the meadow. She taught him to enter the meadow slowly and look for signs of danger. Once it was safe, Bambi ran through the green grass and jumped over streams. It felt wonderful to be so free!

Bambi met other deer for the first time, including a playful young fawn called Faline. He also saw a mighty buck known as the Great Prince of the Forest. Bambi thought his antlers seemed to reach the sky. The Prince was Bambi's father!

Bambi awoke one winter morning and found something cold and white covering the forest floor. He had never seen snow before. Bambi heard it crunch beneath his hooves as he walked through the woods. He saw Thumper sliding on the frozen pond. "It's all right," Thumper assured him, "the water's stiff!"

Once the snows melted, the first flowers of spring appeared. The animals had changed over winter. Bambi had grown the antlers of a young buck, and Thumper and Flower looked different, too. Even the birds were acting strangely.

Friend Owl said the birds were twitterpated—they had fallen in love. It didn't take long for it to happen to Flower and Thumper! Bambi told himself he'd never do that. He walked on alone until he heard a familiar voice. It was Faline! Suddenly Bambi was twitterpated, too! From then on, Bambi and Faline were always together.

One day Bambi noticed a strange smell in the forest—
smoke! He raced through the woods, warning the others
about the raging fire. When Bambi grew tired, the Great
Prince appeared and urged him on. There was no time
to waste!

The animals swam to the safety of a river
island. Once the last fire burned out, they
returned to the forest to rebuild their homes.
Eventually springtime arrived again, and
Thumper and his babies were back at Friend
Owl's tree. This time the news was about
Faline—she'd given birth to twins!

Bambi proudly stood on the rocks nearby. It was his turn to rule the forest now. As he watched his father disappear into the woods, Bambi knew he would teach his children to be brave and wise, just as the Great Prince had taught him.

The Lion King

Adapted by Kate Hannigan
Illustrated by the Disney Storybook Artists

On a sunny morning on the great plains of Africa, the animals gathered to welcome the Lion King's cub into the world. They knew Simba would one day be king. Only Scar, King Mufasa's brother, refused to celebrate. He was angry that he would never rule the Pride Lands.

As Simba grew, his father taught him the ways of the kingdom. "We are all connected in the circle of life," said Mufasa. He also explained that Simba would rule everything the light touched—only the shadowy place was forbidden.

Scar wanted to make trouble for Simba, so he told his nephew lies about the shadowy place. He said that only the bravest lions went there.

Simba wanted to be brave like his father, so he ran with his friend Nala to the shadowy place. Zazu, Mufasa's assistant, followed them. As they looked all around, something moved in the shadows. Hyenas! Simba and Nala tried to run away, but they were trapped. At the last moment, Mufasa let out a mighty roar and chased the hyenas away.

Scar was angry that the cubs had escaped, so he devised another terrible plan to make himself the Lion King. Scar led Simba into a deep gorge and told him to wait for a special surprise. Simba waited and waited. Finally he heard a low rumble and saw the ground begin to shake. At Scar's command, the hyenas had caused a stampede of wildebeests. And they were coming right at him!

Simba scrambled to get out of the way. Suddenly, Mufasa appeared and carried him to safety. Simba was unhurt, but his father was not so lucky. Simba called after him, but Mufasa did not answer.

Scar wanted to chase Simba from the Pride Lands, so he blamed his nephew for Mufasa's accident.

"Run away, Simba, and never come back!" said the wicked Scar.

Simba was frightened, and he ran and ran. He didn't stop until he was deep in the desert. Two friendly animals, a meerkat named Timon and a warthog called Pumbaa, found Simba and gave him water. They taught him hakuna matata: "no worries."

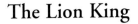

Simba stayed with his
new friends and tried to
forget the past. He grew
bigger and stronger and
looked more like his
father every day.

One afternoon,
Timon and Pumbaa
were searching for food
when they saw a lion
hunting for her lunch. It
was Simba's old friend, Nala.
She told Simba how terrible
things were under Scar's rule.
Nala said Simba was their only hope
to save the Pride Lands.

Simba raced back to the Pride Lands in search of his uncle. When Scar saw Simba, he thought the powerful lion was Mufasa back to haunt him. Scar ordered his hyenas to attack, but the lions protected Simba and chased the hyenas away. Scar and Simba battled fiercely up and down the rocks.

After a long fight, Simba forced Scar to admit what had happened so many years ago. Scar told the lions it was his fault — not Simba's — that Mufasa was gone.

Simba chased Scar away forever. Finally he was able to take his rightful place as the Lion King.

Slowly Simba climbed to the top of Pride Rock, remembering all that his father had taught him. The animals cheered once again, this time welcoming Simba and Nala's cub into the world. A new circle of life was begun.

The Rescuers

Adapted by Lora Kalkman
Illustrated by the Disney Storybook Artists

Mice from all over the world gathered for a meeting. It was a special meeting of the Rescue Aid Society. The society leader announced that someone was in distress.

Bernard, the society janitor, retrieved a note from inside a green bottle that had washed ashore. The note was from a little girl named Penny. She needed help.

A very pretty mouse named Bianca asked for the assignment. She really wanted to find and rescue Penny.

Many mice offered to assist Bianca, for they were all fond of her. Bianca surprised everyone when she asked Bernard to help.

"M-m-me?" stammered Bernard, who seemed quite wary. "I'm only a janitor."

Bianca smiled and assured him he would do a fine job. Reluctantly, Bernard agreed to accompany her on the mission.

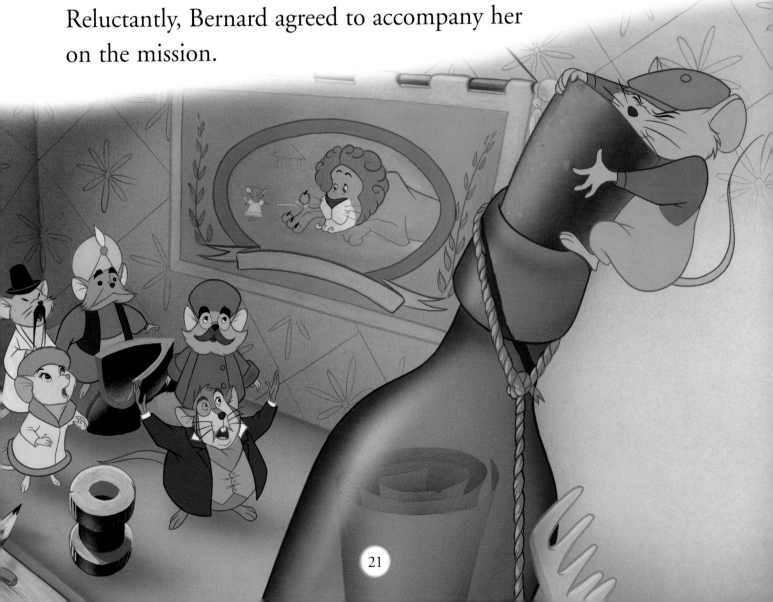

There was just one clue to Penny's whereabouts. The note in the bottle was addressed to Morningside Orphanage. Bernard and Bianca quickly made their way across town. When they arrived at the orphanage, they did not find Penny. Instead, they were startled by Rufus, a kind old cat.

Bernard and Bianca inquired about Penny. Rufus explained that she had disappeared. A mean woman named Medusa had offered Penny a ride once, he said. But Penny had been smart and refused.

Bernard and Bianca raced to Medusa's pawn shop down the street. Inside, they overheard Medusa talking on the telephone with her assistant, Snoops. Bianca gasped when she heard Medusa mention a little girl. Soon it was clear that Medusa had kidnapped Penny! She had taken Penny to Devil's Bayou where Snoops was guarding her.

Bernard and Bianca knew they had to get to the swamp right away.

Bernard and Bianca went to the airport. They climbed aboard Orville, a large white albatross. After a rather bumpy ride, they arrived at Devil's Bayou. They were greeted by friendly swamp mice.

Just then, Bernard and Bianca saw Medusa's two mean alligators. The alligators held Penny, who had tried to escape. The two mice followed the alligators back to Medusa's hideout on an old riverboat.

Bernard and Bianca snuck inside and found Penny. "We're here to rescue you," Bernard announced. But before they could escape, Medusa took Penny to a deep, dark cave. Medusa was forcing Penny to search the cave for a giant diamond called the Devil's Eye.

Bernard and Bianca hid in Penny's pocket and helped her search. Just as the tide came in, Bianca spotted the diamond. With water swirling around them, the courageous trio retrieved the gem and got out just in time.

Everyone returned to the riverboat. Medusa hid the diamond in Penny's teddy bear. Just as Medusa was about to get away, the mice tripped her. The teddy bear tumbled across the room. Penny quickly grabbed it and ran.

Meanwhile, the friendly swamp folk had come to help. They attacked Medusa and Snoops so Penny could get away. Bernard and Bianca lured the alligators into a trap. Then everyone raced to Medusa's swampmobile.

Penny drove the swampmobile through the bayou, but Medusa was not far behind. She was determined to get the diamond. Luckily, Penny was a good driver. With one quick turn, she sent Medusa and her alligators crashing into the riverboat. Penny and all the mice got away.

Penny gave the Devil's Eye to a museum. Then she received the greatest reward of all. She was adopted by a mommy and daddy who loved her very much.

Peter Pan

Adapted by Kate Hannigan
Illustrated by the Disney Storybook Artists

Every night at bedtime in a cozy house in London, Wendy, John, and Michael Darling told stories of the brave Peter Pan and a magical place called Never Land. The children believed Peter Pan was a real person, and they made him the hero of their games. Their mother believed Peter Pan was the spirit of youth.

Peter Pan liked Wendy's stories and listened to them outside the nursery window. He knew everyone there believed in him. Everyone, that is, except Wendy's father. One night, he'd had enough of Wendy's wild stories and said it was time she grew up. "This will be your last night in the nursery," Father said.

After the children had drifted off to sleep, there was a sound at the window. It was Peter Pan! He and Tinker Bell were searching for Peter's shadow.

Peter found his shadow in a dresser drawer, and Wendy stitched it onto the tips of his toes. This way, he would never lose it again.

Peter was angry when he heard it was Wendy's last night in the nursery. Peter asked the children to fly with him to Never Land, where no one ever had to grow up.

Wendy and the boys thought Never Land sounded wonderful, so they joined Peter and Tinker Bell and soared over London. They flew on and on to Peter's magical home.

Once they reached Never Land, they rested on a cloud high above Pirate's Cove, where Captain Hook's ship was waiting.

Captain Hook was always after Peter, and he fired a cannon right at them. Peter told Tinker Bell to take the children to safety with the Lost Boys. But Tinker Bell was jealous, and she told the Lost Boys to knock Wendy from the sky.

Peter charged Tinker Bell with high treason and banished her from the island forever. That sounded a bit harsh to Wendy, so Peter made it just a week instead.

Tinker Bell flew away all alone as Peter and the children explored Never Land. Michael and John played follow the leader with the Lost Boys, and Peter took Wendy to see Mermaid Lagoon.

Before long, Captain Hook caught Tinker Bell and tricked her into revealing Peter's hideout. Tinker Bell made Captain Hook promise not to lay a hand — or a hook! — on Peter.

Hook and his pirates rushed to Peter's hideout and laid a trap. As Wendy, her brothers, and the Lost Boys tried to leave, Hook captured them and carried them back to the pirate ship. Hook made them walk the plank.

"Peter Pan will save us," Wendy said confidently.

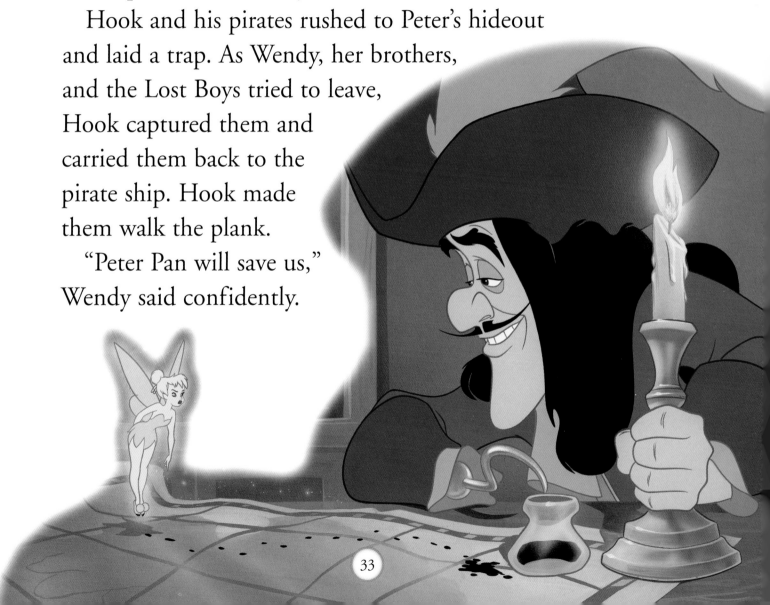

Tinker Bell told Peter Pan what had happened, and they raced to Hook's pirate ship. Peter caught Wendy in his arms just before she fell into the water. Then he freed John, Michael, and the Lost Boys to fight the pirates while he battled Captain Hook.

They ran up and down the ship until Hook fell overboard into the water, where a hungry crocodile was waiting.

Finally it was time for the children to return home, and they set sail with Peter Pan on Captain Hook's ship.

With a sprinkling of Tinker Bell's pixie dust, the ship turned to gold and soared through the night sky back to London.

Wendy's parents found her asleep at the nursery window. She awoke and looked up at the moon and Peter Pan's pirate ship sailing across it. Her father stared. He told Wendy he'd seen that ship before—long ago, when he was very young.

Toy Story 2

Adapted by Lisa Harkrader
Illustrated by DiCicco Studios

Woody was a cowboy doll. He was Andy's favorite toy. But when Andy went to summer camp, Woody had to stay home.

While Andy was gone, Andy's mom held a garage sale. She gathered some of Andy's old toys to sell. When Woody tried to save one of the toys, he ended up on a table in the garage sale, too.

Soon a car pulled up. A man named Al got out. When Al saw Woody, he tried to buy him.

"Oh, no," said Andy's mom. "Woody isn't for sale. He shouldn't even be out here."

Al waited till Andy's mom wasn't looking. Then he snatched Woody and ran to his car.

Buzz, Andy's space ranger toy, tried to save Woody. Buzz ran after the car, but it zoomed away.

LZTYBRN

Al took Woody to his apartment. He put Woody on a shelf. Then Al left and locked the door behind him.

Woody saw that he was not alone. Three other toys — a horse, a cowgirl, and an old prospector — sat on the shelf beside him.

"Woody!" said the cowgirl.

"You know me?" said Woody.

"Of course we do," said the cowgirl. She turned the television on so Woody could see an old TV program. Woody was the star. Bullseye was his horse. Jessie the cowgirl and the Prospector were his friends.

Woody, Bullseye, Jessie, and the Prospector were all part of a collectible toy set. Al had looked for Woody for a long time. Now that he had Woody, Al was going to sell the set to a toy museum in Japan. Woody would never see Andy again.

Buzz told the other toys about the man who had taken Woody. He told them the license plate on the man's car said LZTYBRN. The toys tried to figure out what LZTYBRN meant. "I know!" said Buzz. "It means Al's Toy Barn." Buzz, Hamm, Rex, and Mr. Potato Head vaulted out of Andy's room on Slinky's coiled spring. The five toys set off toward Al's Toy Barn to rescue Woody.

When they got to the toy store, they couldn't find Woody. But they did find Al working in his office. When Al left the store, Buzz, Hamm, Rex, Mr. Potato Head, and Slinky were right behind him. They followed Al home. They raced upstairs and crept into his apartment through a vent. There they found Woody.

But Woody refused to go with them. "I can't leave Jessie, Bullseye, and the Prospector," he said.

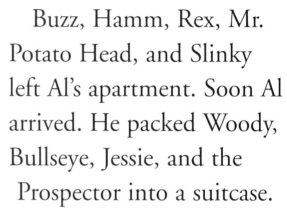

Buzz, Hamm, Rex, Mr. Potato Head, and Slinky left Al's apartment. Soon Al arrived. He packed Woody, Bullseye, Jessie, and the Prospector into a suitcase. Buzz and the other toys saw Al put the suitcase into his car and drive off. "He's taking them to Japan!" said Buzz.

Buzz and the other toys followed Al to the airport. They saved Woody and Bullseye, but Jessie and the Prospector were still stuck in the suitcase. Buzz and Woody climbed onto Bullseye's back and galloped after the suitcase. They rescued Jessie, but the Prospector refused to come with them. He wanted to live in the museum in Japan.

Buzz, Woody, and the other toys took Jessie and Bullseye home. When Andy returned from camp, all his toys, including his new toys, Jessie and Bullseye, were waiting to welcome him.

The Fox and the Hound

Adapted by Alicia Shems

Illustrated by the Disney Storybook Artists

It was a lush, green early summer, and the baby animals were still living with their mothers. All except one — a baby fox sat alone and scared under a fence. Help came when Big Mama the owl, Boomer the woodpecker, and Dinky the sparrow called on Widow Tweed. The kind widow carried the fox home and cared for him. She named him Tod.

A hunter named Amos Slade lived next door with his hound dog puppy, Copper. One day, Copper smelled a new scent. It was Tod, who had wandered into the yard. The two quickly became fast friends. Tod and Copper played together all summer long. One sunny day, Tod and Copper pledged to be friends forever.

Amos finally had to leash Copper to his barrel so that the puppy would not stray from home. Tod missed Copper and went to visit. Copper was happy to see his friend, but he knew that Amos would not want him to play with a fox.

Tod, however, was curious about Chief, Amos's old hunting dog. Copper warned Tod not to disturb Chief, but Tod accidentally woke up the old dog. And when Chief smelled the fox, the chase was on! Widow Tweed saved Tod, but the friends now knew that playing together was nearly impossible.

When the autumn leaves began to change colors, Amos took Copper and Chief away on a long hunting trip. Tod was lonely all through the long, cold winter. He thought wistfully of his friend Copper.

When spring arrived, Copper, Chief, and Amos returned home. Overjoyed, Tod went to visit his friend. But things had changed. Though they were still friends, Copper was now a hunting dog—one who was supposed to hunt foxes. And Tod was a full-grown fox.

Amos Slade didn't like Tod one bit. He thought that foxes should be hunted, not kept as pets. The widow couldn't let Tod outside, for fear that Chief would get him. But she didn't want to keep him cooped up inside, either. So Widow Tweed drove Tod to a game preserve where he could live in the wild, free and safe.

Tod was lonely again. And once again Big Mama came to his rescue by introducing him to Vixey, a pretty female fox.

Vixey taught him about the forest, and Tod entertained Vixey with his games. Before long, they fell in love.

One day, no-good Amos sneaked into the game preserve to hunt. By accident, he and Copper disturbed a bear. Tod remembered his pledge to be Copper's friend always, and courageously ran to their rescue.

After the struggle with the bear, Copper could no longer hide his friendship with Tod. The love between the two animals softened Amos's heart, and Amos let Tod go.

The friends knew they had to part. Tod's home was in the forest with Vixey. Copper's home was with Amos. But in their hearts, the fox and the hound knew they would remain friends forever.

Alice in Wonderland

Adapted by Kate Hannigan
Illustrated by the Disney Storybook Artists

One beautiful afternoon, a curious little girl named Alice sat on the branch of a big tree and listened to her sister read aloud from a book. Alice wasn't the least bit interested, so she began to drift off into her imagination.

Suddenly a white rabbit dashed by wearing a jacket and tie. He was carrying a large pocket watch. "I'm late! I'm late! For a very important date," he said. Alice thought the White Rabbit might be late for something fun, like a party. So she chased after him and fell down a rabbit hole.

When Alice reached the bottom, she saw the rabbit scurry through a small door. The doorknob told Alice she was too big to get through. He suggested she drink from the bottle on the table. With every sip Alice took, she shrank smaller and smaller.

DRINK ME

Alice was just the right size to pass through the door, but it was locked. She saw the key on the table high above her. The doorknob suggested she eat some cookies. With each bite, Alice grew bigger and bigger. She grew so tall, she bumped her head on the ceiling!

The doorknob laughed, but Alice began to cry. Her tears were giant drops that flooded the room. Alice sipped from the bottle again and shrank small enough to climb into it. She floated right through the keyhole.

On the other side of the door, Alice saw talking birds, dancing fish, and lots of strange things. Soon she stumbled into twins called Tweedledee and Tweedledum. They gave Alice a lesson about manners.

Alice saw the White Rabbit hurry past, but she was too tiny to catch him. Pushing aside tall blades of grass, she followed him into the woods.

Alice entered a wonderful garden where giant butterflies fluttered by. She noticed their wings were slices of bread. A rose told her they were bread-and-butterflies. When the flowers realized Alice wasn't a flower, they chased her from the garden. "She's nothing but a common weed!" they said. Alice thought they could use a lesson in manners.

Nibbling on mushrooms, Alice grew to just the right size. Soon she came across the Mad Hatter and the March Hare having a tea party, so she joined them. There were teapots and teacups everywhere. Alice really wanted a cup of tea, but they made her feel very unwelcome at their un-birthday party.

"We have only one birthday a year," they explained. "But there are 364 un-birthdays!" Alice said it was her un-birthday, too, so they gave her a cake with a big candle.

Exasperated, Alice gave up searching for the White Rabbit. Just then, he appeared and announced the arrival of the Queen of Hearts and her king. Alice joined the Queen for a game of croquet. The Cheshire Cat appeared, too, and played a trick on the Queen. She thought Alice had done it. "Off with her head!" she screeched. Alice wanted to go home— right away. She began to run and run. When she looked behind her, the Mad Hatter, the March Hare, and all the creatures she had met were chasing after her.

Finally, she heard a familiar voice. "Alice, what are you talking about?" her sister asked. Alice opened her eyes. She had been dreaming! She picked up her cat and scratched its ears. Alice thought it was a fine time to go home and have a cup of tea.

Pinocchio

Adapted by Kate Hannigan
Illustrated by the Disney Storybook Artists

On a quiet night in a sleepy village, the old woodcarver Geppetto put the finishing touches on his wooden puppet. He smiled at the toy and decided to call it Pinocchio. As Geppetto climbed into bed that night, he thought Pinocchio looked almost alive. Wouldn't that be nice, he thought to himself. And gazing up at the starry night sky, Geppetto made a wish.

Suddenly a bright light filled the room, and the Blue Fairy appeared. She tapped Pinocchio with her magic wand and brought him to life. "Prove yourself brave, truthful, and unselfish, and someday you will be a real boy," she said.

The fairy told Pinocchio he would have to choose between right and wrong and follow his conscience. Pinocchio didn't know what a conscience was, so the fairy asked Jiminy Cricket to help.

When Geppetto awoke and found Pinocchio walking and talking, he danced for joy. He sent Pinocchio off to school just like a real child. Pinocchio skipped along excitedly, carrying his books and a shiny red apple.

Soon he met a sly fox named Foulfellow and a cat called Gideon who told Pinocchio he should work in the theater. Jiminy Cricket tried to convince him to stay in school, but Pinocchio didn't listen.

The evil puppeteer, Stromboli,
greedily clapped his hands when he met Pinocchio.
This puppet with no strings would make him a fortune!
Stromboli locked Pinocchio up so he couldn't escape. Even
Jiminy couldn't free him.

Finally the Blue Fairy appeared. She asked Pinocchio why
he didn't go to school, and he told her a lie. Suddenly his
nose began to grow. With each lie, his nose grew longer until
birds nested on it.

Once Pinocchio promised to stop telling lies, the Blue Fairy freed him. Pinocchio and Jiminy Cricket raced back to Geppetto. But on the way home, Pinocchio ran into Foulfellow again.

This time, the sly fox told Pinocchio about a place called Pleasure Island, where boys could be lazy and skip school. There was a coach leaving at midnight.

Pinocchio thought it sounded like fun, and he hopped on board and met a friend called Lampwick. "Being bad is a lot of fun," Pinocchio told Lampwick. The boys made all sorts of mischief until suddenly they sprouted donkey ears.

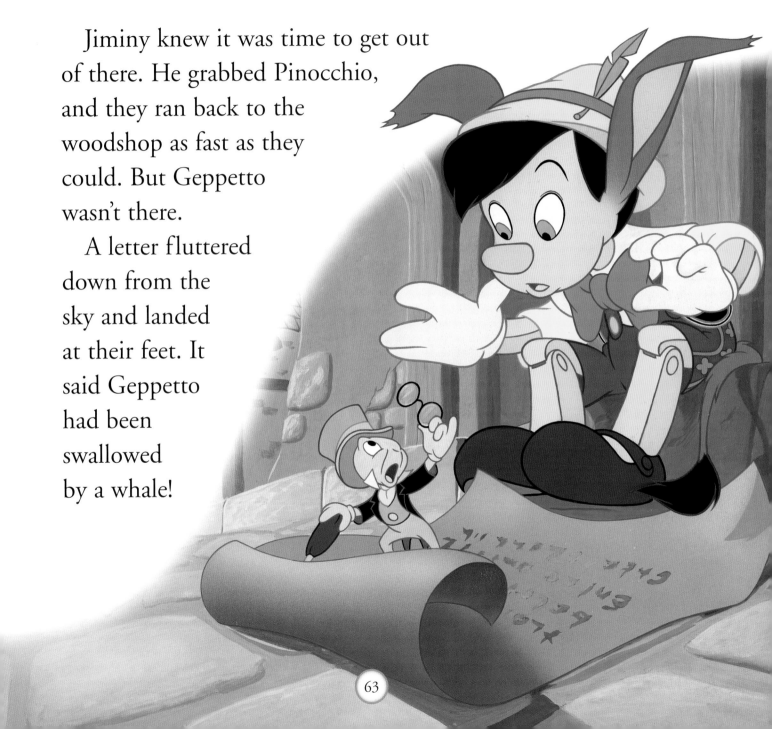

Jiminy knew it was time to get out of there. He grabbed Pinocchio, and they ran back to the woodshop as fast as they could. But Geppetto wasn't there.

A letter fluttered down from the sky and landed at their feet. It said Geppetto had been swallowed by a whale!

Pinocchio and Jiminy Cricket swam to the bottom of the ocean in search of Geppetto. Finally they found him trapped in the belly of a whale called Monstro. But how could they escape? "We'll make the whale sneeze," Pinocchio said.

Pinocchio and Geppetto started a fire with thick, black smoke. When Monstro sneezed, they shot right out of his mouth and swam for safety. Geppetto quickly grew tired and told Pinocchio to save himself. But Pinocchio couldn't leave his father. He pulled Geppetto to the shore, and then he collapsed in exhaustion.

Geppetto carried Pinocchio home and laid him on the bed. The Blue Fairy appeared again. She had seen Pinocchio save his father's life. He really was brave, truthful, and unselfish. With the wave of her wand, she brought the wooden puppet back to life. Finally, Pinocchio was a real boy.

The Hunchback of Notre Dame

Adapted by Lisa Harkrader
Illustrated by DiCicco Studios

Quasimodo looked down on the Festival of Fools. He longed to be part of the music and dancing. But Quasimodo had never been outside the Cathedral of Notre Dame. He was the bell ringer at the huge church, and he had spent his whole life high in the bell tower. His master, Frollo, would not let him leave. Quasimodo's back was hunched and his face twisted. Frollo said nobody outside the cathedral would accept him. So Quasimodo stayed in the cathedral and carved wooden miniatures of the city he had never visited.

But Quasimodo was tired of being alone in the tower. He climbed over the balcony and swung down on a rope to the festival.

Quasimodo loved the festival. Nobody noticed his hunched back or his twisted face. They just thought he was wearing a mask. Quasimodo especially loved watching a gypsy named Esmeralda, who was a wonderful dancer. Esmeralda pulled Quasimodo onto the stage and crowned him King of Fools. The crowd cheered. But Frollo's soldiers didn't cheer. They threw tomatoes and tried to hurt Quasimodo. Esmeralda helped Quasimodo escape.

Frollo was watching. He was angry at Esmeralda. He didn't like gypsies, and he didn't want anyone to help Quasimodo. He wanted Quasimodo to learn a lesson. Frollo ordered Phoebus, his Captain of the Guard, to arrest Esmeralda.

But Phoebus liked Esmeralda. He wanted to help her. She was kind and beautiful, and she hadn't done anything wrong.

Esmeralda dashed inside the Cathedral of Notre Dame, where she knew she would be safe. Phoebus and Frollo both followed her.

"Arrest the gypsy girl!" Frollo cried.

"I can't," said Phoebus. "She's in a church."

No one could arrest Esmeralda while she was in the cathedral. She could only be arrested if she went outside the safe walls of Notre Dame. So Frollo placed guards at each entrance. If Esmeralda tried to leave, the guards would take her prisoner.

Quasimodo led Esmeralda to the bell tower. He showed her his carvings of the city. Esmeralda liked Quasimodo and she loved his carvings, but she couldn't live in the bell tower forever. She had to escape. Quasimodo told her he knew a way out. He carried her over the balcony and helped her slide down the roof.

When they reached the street below, Esmeralda gave Quasimodo a woven band. She told Quasimodo that if he ever needed her, the band would help him find her. Then Esmeralda disappeared into the night.

When Frollo found that Esmeralda had escaped, he was furious. He told Quasimodo and Phoebus that he knew where the gypsies were hiding. His soldiers would attack them at dawn.

Quasimodo and Phoebus had to warn Esmeralda. They realized that the woven band she'd given Quasimodo was a map. They used the map to find the gypsy hiding place. But Frollo and his soldiers followed them. The soldiers arrested Esmeralda and took her back to the city square. And Frollo chained Quasimodo inside the bell tower.

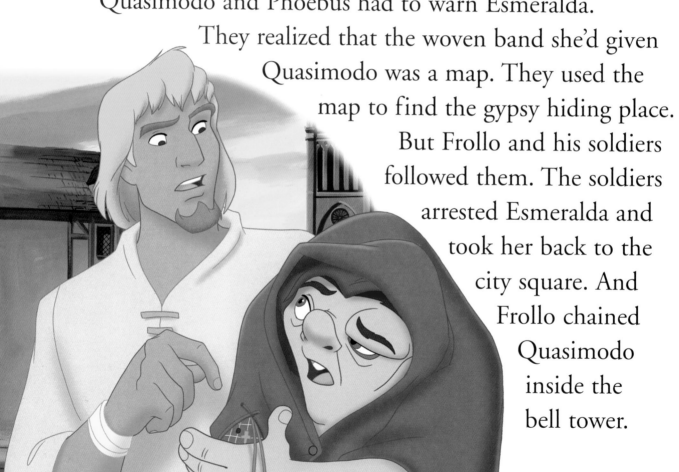

Quasimodo broke the chains and climbed down to the square. He rescued Esmeralda and carried her away. Frollo was angrier than ever. He followed them up to the bell tower. But when he tried to catch Quasimodo, Frollo fell from the tower.

The people cheered. They loved Quasimodo. He had saved them from the evil Frollo.

The Aristocats

Adapted by Lora Kalkman
Illustrated by the Disney Storybook Artists

Duchess was a beautiful white Persian cat. She and her three kittens lived in a big, beautiful mansion in Paris. Their owner, Madame Adelaide, was a grand old lady who loved her cats dearly. She and her butler, Edgar, treated the cats very well.

One day Madame's lawyer came to visit. Madame asked him to prepare a will. She intended to leave her entire vast fortune to the cats. Madame added that once the cats' lifetimes were over, the fortune would belong to Edgar.

It just so happened that Edgar overheard Madame. He was very upset to learn the cats would inherit everything first. He wanted the fortune for himself, and he did not want to wait.

Edgar devised a sneaky plan. That night, he put sleeping potion in the cats' cream. After Duchess and the kittens enjoyed their treat, they all fell into a deep sleep.

Edgar put the sleeping cats in a basket. He climbed aboard his motorbike and drove to the country. Edgar planned to leave the cats there so he could collect Madame's fortune all the sooner.

When Edgar was startled by two dogs, the basket fell from the motorbike. It landed under a bridge.

Upon waking, the cats were surprised to find themselves in the country. Duchess made sure the kittens were safe. Then they tried to determine what happened.

"Edgar did this to us," declared Toulouse, who had caught a sleepy glimpse of the greedy butler. The others couldn't believe it.

When it started to rain, the cats climbed into the basket for the night.

The next day, an orange alley cat happened by. The
alley cat, named Thomas O'Malley, thought Duchess was
wonderful. The two cats talked and flirted, and O'Malley
offered to help Duchess get back to Paris.

When O'Malley found out that Duchess had three kittens,
he had second thoughts. He didn't want any kittens cramping
his swingin' style. But as he watched the family walk slowly
away, he decided to help after all.

First O'Malley helped them
all aboard a truck. They rode
for a while, until the driver
chased them away Then they
walked, encountering many
interesting characters along
the way.

That night, Duchess and the kittens spent a rollicking evening with O'Malley and his alley cat friends. They had a splendid time.

Duchess and O'Malley wished they could stay together. But Duchess knew they had to return to Madame, who must have missed them dearly.

Edgar was dismayed when he discovered Duchess and the kittens had returned. Before Madame even knew they were home, Edgar devised another sneaky plan. He put the cats in a sack and took them to the barn. Then he put them in a crate to be shipped to Timbuktu.

Fortunately, the cats had many friends at Madame's. Roquefort the mouse ran to tell O'Malley that the cats were in trouble. After sending Roquefort to find his alley cat friends, O'Malley hurried to the barn.

O'Malley and the horse tried to save Duchess and the kittens, but they needed help. Luckily, Roquefort and the alley cats arrived just in time.

Working together, they forced Edgar into the crate. Then Edgar was shipped to Timbuktu!

After that, Madame let Thomas O'Malley and all of his friends live in the mansion, too. They all lived happily ever after.

Robin Hood

Adapted by Lora Kalkman
Illustrated by the Disney Storybook Artists

Robin Hood and Little John were considered heroes to most people. They robbed from the rich to give to the poor. Normally, stealing is wrong, of course; everyone knows that. But evil Prince John made poor people pay enormously unfair taxes. Robin Hood and Little John just took the money back and returned it to its rightful owners.

The taxes were usually collected by the sheriff. The Sheriff of Nottingham was especially rotten. He even took children's birthday money to give to Prince John!

One day, Robin Hood and Little John noticed Prince John's carriage approaching Nottingham. They devised a plan. They dressed up as fortune tellers and enticed Prince John to have his fortune told. As Robin Hood gazed into a pretend crystal ball, he swiped the prince's gold.

Outside, Little John swiped even more.

When Prince John realized what had happened, he was outraged. But instead of yelling, all he could do was whimper "Mommy," in a baby voice. Then he sucked his thumb. He knew he'd been hoodwinked by Robin Hood!

The prince summoned the Sheriff of Nottingham for help. They decided to hold an archery contest in order to capture Robin Hood. To make sure he would attend, the prince announced that first prize would be a kiss from Maid Marian. He knew Robin Hood liked her, for the two used to be sweethearts.

Sure enough, Robin Hood attended the contest. But he came disguised as a stork! At first, no one but Maid Marian recognized the dashing rogue. Everyone cheered for the stranger, who proved to be an excellent archer.

Finally, when the stork made one especially heroic shot, Prince John realized he must be Robin Hood. The chase was on, and a crazy battle ensued. Fortunately, Robin Hood, Little John, and Maid Marian escaped into the woods.

Prince John couldn't believe Robin Hood got away. The townspeople cheered for their hero and poked fun at Prince John. Angry, the wicked prince raised taxes even more. When people could not pay the taxes, they were put in jail. Mean Prince John even put children in jail!

When Friar Tuck dared to speak out against the sheriff, the sheriff put him in jail, too! Then Prince John devised another plan. He announced he would hang Friar Tuck in the morning. He told his guards to capture Robin Hood when he came to rescue Friar Tuck.

Robin Hood

Robin Hood knew he had to act quickly. That night, he and Little John sneaked into the castle. Robin Hood wore another disguise and tricked the sheriff. He took the key to the jail and gave it to Little John, who set everyone free. Meanwhile, Robin Hood took back all the gold from Prince John's room!

Before long, the prince and his guards gave chase. Robin Hood fought the guards while the others escaped. Finally, Robin Hood climbed tall walls, swung from ropes, and swam through a moat to get away.

During the struggle, the sheriff accidentally set fire to the castle. When Prince John saw the castle in flames, he could do nothing but whimper "Mommy," and suck his thumb some more.

The townspeople were happy to have their gold back. They were even happier to learn of King Richard's return. The king had been away, fighting in a war. But the war ended, and King Richard came back. He locked up the sheriff, Prince John, and all of the prince's helpers.

Meanwhile, Robin Hood and Maid Marian had a joyous wedding. All of the townspeople were invited to the celebration.

Nottingham was a happy place once again.

Atlantis

Adapted by Lisa Harkrader
Illustrated by Sue DiCicco and Andrew Williamson

Milo Thatch dreamed of finding the lost city of Atlantis. According to legend, Atlantis was the home of an advanced civilization, but it had disappeared into the ocean thousands of years ago. Milo worked for a large museum. He tried to convince the museum directors to send him on an expedition to find Atlantis, but they only laughed at him.

A very rich man named Whitmore sent for Milo. He gave Milo a book called *The Shepherd's Journal*. It was written in an ancient language, and it explained how to get to Atlantis. Whitmore asked Milo to use *The Shepherd's Journal* to lead a crew on an expedition to find the lost city. Milo agreed, and the crew began its journey.

As the expedition's submarine cruised through the ocean, Milo decoded *The Shepherd's Journal*. He told Rourke, the captain of the expedition, how to find the underwater tunnel that led to Atlantis. He also warned Rourke to be careful. According to the *Journal,* a huge monster called the Leviathan guarded the entrance to the tunnel.

When the submarine reached the tunnel, the Leviathan attacked. Rourke, Milo, and the crew escaped in subpods.

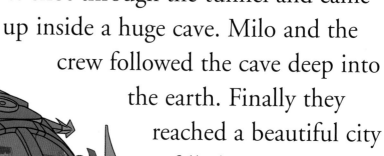

The small submarines shot through the tunnel and came up inside a huge cave. Milo and the crew followed the cave deep into the earth. Finally they reached a beautiful city filled with birds, trees, and waterfalls. They had found Atlantis!

A group of Atlantean warriors met them at the edge of the city. One of the warriors was the princess of Atlantis, Kida. She trusted Milo. Her city was dying, and she needed Milo's help. She led Milo to an ancient inscription. She asked Milo to read the inscription and tell her how to save Atlantis.

The inscription described an ancient crystal that would keep the city alive. But when Milo and Kida searched for the crystal, Rourke took them captive. Rourke wanted to sell the crystal and become rich.

Rourke forced Milo to lead him to the crystal. The crystal glowed with a strange light. When the light shone on Kida, she became part of it. Rourke grabbed the crystallized Kida and set off. But his crew refused to go with him. When Milo chased after Rourke, the crew went along to help.

Rourke tried to escape in a hot air balloon. Milo leaped onto the balloon. He grabbed a broken piece of the crystal and slashed at Rourke. When the crystal touched Rourke's skin, Rourke himself became a crystal and shattered into bits.

The crystal released Kida. It rose into the sky, and the dying city came back to life. When the crew left to go home, Milo stayed behind with Kida. He wanted to live in Atlantis, the city he'd dreamed of all his life.

Lady and the Tramp

Adapted by Kate Hannigan
Illustrated by the Disney Storybook Artists

Lady was a beautiful dog with big brown eyes and a honey-colored coat. She lived with Jim Dear and Darling, and they loved her very much.

One day, Lady met a happy-go-lucky dog named Tramp. He didn't have a family to take care of, so he wandered around town and did whatever he pleased.

When Tramp heard that Lady's humans were going to have a baby, he warned Lady. Babies change everything, Tramp said. Lady was worried. She wasn't even sure what a baby was. But when it finally arrived, Lady took one look at the tiny baby and fell in love. Now she had three humans to care for!

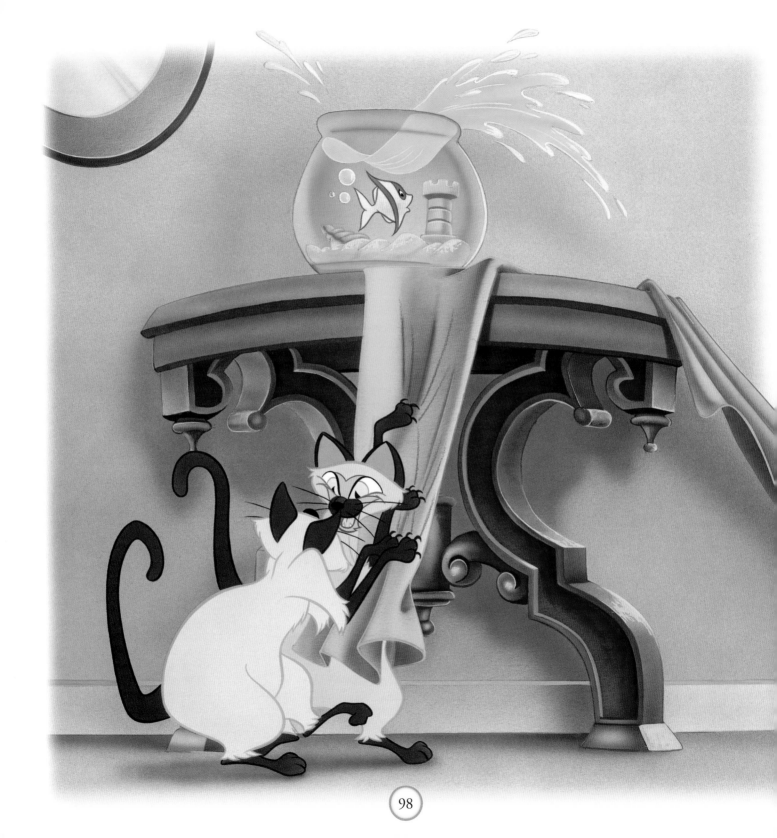

Before long, Jim Dear and Darling had to take a trip. Aunt Sarah came to help take care of the new baby. She brought boxes, bags, and a big suitcase, but that wasn't all. She brought her two Siamese cats, too! The cats were nothing but trouble for Lady. They knocked over vases, tipped over the fishbowl, and made a mess of everything.

Lady barked and barked, trying to control them. But Aunt Sarah didn't understand. She took Lady down to the pet store and bought a muzzle. Lady couldn't bear it! She ran from the store and down the street as fast as her legs could carry her.

A pack of mean dogs began to chase Lady. She was scared. "Leave her alone!" shouted Tramp. He jumped in front of the ferocious dogs and chased them away.

Tramp saved Lady's life.

Tramp helped Lady get the muzzle off. Finally, Lady was free! They decided to celebrate at Tramp's favorite restaurant.

The owner served them a special dinner of spaghetti and meatballs. He even set a fancy table and played music. Lady and Tramp fell in love.

The next morning, Tramp wanted to have some fun. They chased some squawking chickens all around a yard, making quite a ruckus!

Suddenly the dogcatcher appeared. He caught Lady and sent her to the dog pound. Luckily, Lady didn't have to stay there for too long.

Once Lady returned home, Aunt Sarah made her sleep outside in the doghouse. Lady was tied to a chain. When a rat sneaked into the house, Lady tried to chase it. Tramp heard her barking and ran to help. The rat ran into the baby's room!

Lady broke free of her chain and helped Tramp save the baby from the awful rat.

Aunt Sarah heard the dogs barking and promptly called the dogcatcher. The truck came to take Tramp to the dog pound. As Tramp was being led away, Jim Dear and Darling returned home. They ran to the baby's room to see what all the fuss was about.

"Lady, I think you and your friend were trying to save our baby from this rat!" said Jim Dear. They had to hurry and save Tramp.

Lady and Jim Dear jumped into the car and chased after the dogcatcher. Lady's friends Jock and Trusty helped, too. They rescued Tramp just in time.

Before long, Tramp settled down with Lady. He liked having a family to take care of. He and Lady were busy watching over Jim Dear, Darling, and their baby. But that wasn't the only family. Lady and Tramp had four puppies of their own to care for, too!

The Jungle Book

Adapted by Kate Hannigan
Illustrated by the Disney Storybook Artists

Deep in the jungle, a black panther named Bagheera discovered a baby in a basket. But this was no animal baby … it was a man-cub! Bagheera needed to find someone to care for it. He knew of a family of wolves with young cubs. Surely they could take one more mouth to feed, Bagheera thought. And that is how Mowgli came to be raised as a cub in the wolf pack.

Ten rainy seasons passed, and Mowgli grew into a boy. The wolves loved him, but they were afraid Shere Khan would find him soon. The great tiger did not want Man in his jungle, and the wolves were afraid they could not protect Mowgli from him.

Bagheera said he knew of a man-village where Mowgli would be safe. So one night, the two set off through the jungle.

When the man-cub grew too tired to walk any farther, Mowgli and Bagheera slept in the thick branches of a tree. Just as they were drifting off to sleep, Kaa the snake appeared. Kaa was hungry and thought Mowgli would make a tasty morsel. He stared into Mowgli's eyes and hypnotized him! Bagheera woke up just in time to save Mowgli from the slithery snake.

Mowgli did not want to leave the jungle. When morning came, he jumped from the tree and joined a parade of elephants passing below. He marched behind the littlest elephant, then stood in line for inspection. "What happened to your trunk?" asked Colonel Hathi, the elephants' leader. Then he realized that Mowgli was a man-cub!

Bagheera tried to lead Mowgli to the man-village, but Mowgli didn't want to go. The panther grew frustrated and told Mowgli he was on his own. "Don't worry about me," Mowgli said.

Soon Mowgli met a friendly bear called Baloo. Baloo taught Mowgli how to search for bananas and growl like a bear. They had a wonderful time climbing trees and splashing in the river. As they floated lazily downstream, a pack of monkeys watched them from the trees. At the right moment, they reached down and snatched Mowgli right off Baloo's big belly!

Baloo called to Bagheera for help. Together they rescued Mowgli from the monkeys. But now it was clear to Baloo, too — the jungle was no place for the man-cub.

Mowgli was upset when Baloo told him it was time to return to the man-village. He ran away. Bagheera and Baloo searched everywhere, and even asked the elephants for help. As Bagheera talked with Colonel Hathi, Shere Khan listened in the grass nearby. The sly tiger now knew that the man-cub could not be far away. He began his search at once.

All too soon, Shere Khan found Mowgli. "I'm not afraid of you!" Mowgli shouted bravely when he saw the tiger. Shere Khan jumped for Mowgli, but suddenly Baloo appeared. He grabbed Shere Khan's tail and pulled. Some friendly vultures swooped down and carried Mowgli to safety.

Shere Khan and Baloo battled as lightning flashed and started a small fire. Mowgli grabbed a burning branch and tied it to Shere Khan's tail. The tiger, whose only fear was of fire, ran from the jungle and was never heard from again.

Baloo gave Mowgli a big bear hug. Nothing would come between them again, he said. Just then, Mowgli heard a beautiful sound. A girl from the man-village was singing nearby. In an instant, Mowgli fell in love!

Mowgli followed the girl toward the man-village. Bagheera and Baloo waved good-bye. They were sad to see their friend leave. But it was for the best. Mowgli would be safe and at home at last.

Monsters, Inc.

Adapted by Michael John Burns

Illustrated by Judith Holmes Clarke, Caroline Egan, and the Disney Storybook Artists

One fine morning in the city of Monstropolis, Sulley and his roommate Mike began another day of work. They were proud to work at Monsters, Inc., the company that supplied power to the entire city. Sulley and Mike made their way to the busy Scare Floor, where closet doors from all over the world zoomed in on conveyor belts. Scarers like Sulley would go through the doors and scare sleeping children, whose screams were used to power the city. Children's screams were a great source of raw energy in the monster world.

At the end of the day, Sulley was the Top Scarer again. The other monsters congratulated him — all except for slithery Randall, who had a secret plan to be the best.

As Sulley and Mike were leaving, Mike realized that he had forgotten his paperwork. Sulley volunteered to go back to the Scare Floor to get it.

On the dark, quiet Scare Floor, Sulley noticed that someone had left out an active closet door. How terrible! A child could sneak through the door and into the monster world! This would surely mean disaster. It was common monster knowledge that children were highly dangerous.

Carefully, Sulley opened the door and peeked inside. He didn't see any Scarers. Suddenly, he heard a giggle behind him. He turned and saw that a little girl had entered the Scare Floor! Alarmed, Sulley tried to put the little girl back into her room, but she was too fast for him. And in the confusion, Sulley got all tangled up in human toys.

Sulley panicked. After he stashed the evidence of toys, Sulley scooped the little girl into a duffel bag and ran off to find Mike.

Hiding out in their apartment, Mike and Sulley tried to figure out what to do. As they scrambled about, trying to avoid the little girl, Mike tripped and fell down. The little girl laughed. And when she did, power surged. The lights all over town got very bright.

After spending time with the sweet little girl, Sulley slowly came to realize that she wasn't dangerous at all. He found himself growing fond of her. He even gave her a name: Boo.

The next morning Mike and Sulley dressed Boo in a clever monster costume. They planned to sneak her into Monsters, Inc., put her right back into her closet, and send her home.

Back at Monsters, Inc., Sulley and Mike discovered that Randall had a slimy secret plan. Randall had invented a Scream Extractor machine. He planned to solve the energy crisis by stealing children and their screams. Boo was going to be his first victim!

Luckily, Sulley and Mike were able to stop Randall and save Boo. She was sent back home, and her door was destroyed. Sulley would never see Boo again … but at least she was safe.

Months later, Sulley was in charge of Monsters, Inc. He and Mike had discovered that children's laughter was much more powerful than screams. The Scare Floor was now the Laugh Floor. Instead of scaring, monsters told jokes. There was no more energy crisis. But Sulley still missed Boo.

One day, Mike told Sulley he had a surprise for him. It was Boo's door! Mike had put it back together, piece by piece. Excited, Sulley opened the door and peeked inside. He smiled as Boo giggled back at him.

101 Dalmatians

Adapted by Kate Hannigan
Illustrated by the Disney Storybook Artists

Pongo and Perdita lived in a cozy house in London with their two humans, Roger and Anita. One stormy night, Perdita gave birth to puppies. Nanny called to Roger and Pongo and announced the arrival of eight healthy puppies.

"Make that thirteen! No, fourteen!" Nanny shouted again. "Oh, my, fifteen!"

Pongo couldn't believe it. He was the father of fifteen puppies. He danced in delight until the back door burst open.

There at the door stood Anita's old schoolmate, Cruella De Vil. She was excited, too. But she had other plans for Pongo and Perdita's puppies. Cruella wanted to buy them. She pulled out her checkbook and pen, splattering ink all over Roger and Pongo. Roger said they weren't selling the puppies—not a single one. Cruella stormed out of the house in a rage.

One night Pongo and Perdita took a walk in the park with their humans. The house was quiet as Nanny put the puppies to bed. Suddenly there was a knock at the door. Cruella's evil henchmen, Horace and Jasper, pushed their way into the house and stole the puppies.

Roger and Anita tried to help, but it was up to the dogs to find them, Pongo told Perdita. When evening came, they barked an alert to all the dogs of London. They hoped the Twilight Bark would carry their message to someone who could help.

Eventually the message reached a quiet farm in the countryside. An old horse and stray cat heard the alert first. The cat, called Sergeant Tibs, woke up the Colonel, an Old English sheepdog. The Colonel listened. "Fifteen spotted puddles stolen!" he said. Sergeant Tibs said maybe it was puppies, not puddles.

Tibs had heard barking at the old De Vil place nearby. He and the Colonel ran to investigate. Tibs peeked into the house and saw the fifteen missing puppies—and many more puppies that Cruella had bought or stolen. Tibs began to count and count and count. Ninety-nine puppies!

The Colonel barked the news to dogs in a nearby village, and they passed it along. The Twilight Bark carried it all the way back to London. The puppies were found!

Pongo and Perdita ran as fast as they could. They reached the De Vil mansion just in time. Cruella wanted to make fur coats out of the spotted puppies! Pongo and Perdita jumped at Horace and Jasper while Sergeant Tibs and the Colonel led the puppies to safety.

Pongo and Perdita were so happy to see their puppies. But they knew Cruella and her henchmen were still after them!

The dogs ran through the ice and snow until they met a black Labrador, who had arranged a ride back to London. As they waited, the restless puppies rolled in ashes. Pongo told all the puppies to get as dirty as they could. When they were covered in the black soot, they looked like Labradors!

The disguise allowed them to sneak into the waiting van right under Cruella's nose. Water splashed onto the last puppy's back, and Cruella saw his spots. The puppies were escaping! Cruella and her henchmen chased the van. Finally, she crashed into Horace and Jasper's truck.

The puppies made it safely home, and Roger, Anita, and Nanny counted ninety-nine of them. With Pongo and Perdita, that made 101 Dalmatians. "We'll have a plantation," Roger said. "A Dalmatian plantation!" And that's just what they did.

The Black Cauldron

Adapted by Gayla Amaral
Illustrated by the Disney Storybook Artists

Long ago there lived a cruel king whose spirit was captured in a huge black cauldron and hidden for centuries. Evil men searched for the cauldron, knowing that it would give them the power to rule the world!

An old man named Dallben lived in the same land. He had a very special pig, Hen Wen, who could see into the future. A boy named Taran lived with them, too.

One day Hen Wen revealed a frightening image of the Horned King. Dallben knew right away that the Horned King wanted to use Hen Wen to find the Black Cauldron.

"Go!" Dallben ordered Taran. "Take Hen Wen and hide in the forest until I come for you!"

Determined to protect Hen Wen, Taran led him into the Forbidden Forest as Dallben had instructed. As Taran was daydreaming about becoming a famous warrior, he suddenly realized that Hen Wen was missing.

"Hen Wen! Where are you?" called Taran. But instead of Hen Wen, Taran discovered a mischievous creature named Gurgi. Distracted by Gurgi, Taran was unable to find Hen Wen before the little pig was captured by two flying dragons, who whisked him away to the castle of the Horned King.

Overcoming his fears, Taran managed to sneak inside the castle and rescue Hen Wen from the wicked king. Making a mad dash out of the castle, Taran barely had time to throw Hen Wen into the moat.

"Swim! Swim!" he urged Hen Wen. "It's our only chance!" Thankfully, Hen Wen escaped, but Taran was captured and thrown into the castle dungeon.

Deep in the dark dungeon, Taran was surprised to find a
beautiful princess who was also eager to escape. Following her
through the dungeon, he discovered a magic sword in one of
the chambers. Then, hearing a cry for help, they came upon a
minstrel named Fflewddur. As they attempted to set him free,
they were discovered, and had it not been for the
magic sword, they would have been
captured again.

Back in the forest, the trio found Gurgi once again. The furry creature pointed out Hen Wen's tracks, which led them straight to a whirlpool! Down the swirling whirlpool they went, landing in the world of the Fairfolk. As the Fairfolk flitted curiously about, Taran was overjoyed to find Hen Wen there, alive and well.

Taran knew what they must do. "If we destroy the Black Cauldron, it will stop the Horned King," he explained.

The Fairfolk led them to the Black Cauldron — found in the possession of three witches. Trading his sword to the witches in exchange for the cauldron, Taran learned that the only way to destroy the cauldron was to willingly climb inside. Suddenly surrounded by the king's army, they were taken back to the castle. Finally, the Horned King had the Black Cauldron! As the friends despaired, Gurgi suddenly appeared. He courageously threw himself into the cauldron, destroying the king, his army, and the castle. Taran and his friends quickly jumped in a boat and sailed away.

The three witches reappeared, demanding the return of the cauldron. As Fflewddur bargained to exchange it for the sword, Taran sadly stated he would rather have Gurgi instead. No sooner had he uttered the words than Gurgi magically appeared, alive and well — to live happily ever after with his heroic new friends.

Dumbo

Adapted by Kate Hannigan
Illustrated by the Disney Storybook Artists

Mrs. Jumbo the elephant had waited a long, long time for a baby. So the day the stork finally visited, Mrs. Jumbo couldn't have been any happier. There inside the blanket sat the most adorable baby elephant she'd ever seen. He was just perfect!

Mrs. Jumbo smiled proudly as the other elephants fussed over her newborn. Then Jumbo Junior sneezed— *Ah-choo!*—and as he sneezed, his ears flapped open. They were enormous!

136

The elephants laughed and pointed at Baby Jumbo. "Jumbo?" they said. "You mean Dumbo!" Mrs. Jumbo tried to ignore them. She loved Dumbo, big ears and all.

The next morning was the circus parade. The crowds cheered as the animals passed. Dumbo marched in line behind the other elephants. Suddenly he stumbled on his long ears and fell right into the mud.

Everyone laughed at him.

The other elephants thought Dumbo and his big ears were an embarrassment. They turned their backs on Dumbo. "Pretend you don't see him," they said. Dumbo walked away all alone.

Timothy Mouse felt bad for Dumbo. He knew that elephants are afraid of mice, so he walked right over to the giant animals and waved his tiny paws. They were terrified! Timothy laughed and scurried back over to Dumbo. They became fast friends. Timothy liked the little elephant's ears. He thought that Dumbo could be a star.

The next day, the ringmaster announced a new circus act. "Ladies and gentlemen, introducing the elephant pyramid," he said. He wanted Dumbo to leap to the very top of the tower of elephants. But as Dumbo ran toward the teetering tower, he tripped on his long ears and knocked the elephants to the ground.

The elephants were miserable as the circus train chugged home. They raised their trunks and made a promise. "From now on, Dumbo is no longer an elephant!" they said.

The ringmaster felt the same way and made Dumbo perform with the clowns. The crowd laughed and laughed as Dumbo jumped from a tall tower into a tub of water. Dumbo was embarrassed. He didn't want to be a clown—he wanted to be an elephant.

Timothy Mouse was sad for his
friend, and the two settled down in a
haystack for a good night's sleep. Dumbo
dreamed he could fly. He imagined flapping
his ears and soaring like a bird.

When they woke in the morning, Timothy Mouse couldn't
believe his eyes. They were high above the ground in the
branches of a tree! "What happened, Dumbo?" he asked.

Dumbo flapped his ears
like in the dream, but nothing
happened. Finally some birds
hopped over and handed Timothy a black feather. They said
to tell Dumbo it was a magic feather.

It worked! With Timothy perched in his cap, Dumbo
flapped his ears and began to soar into the sky. They flew
above the treetops and all the way back to the circus.

Dumbo

When the clowns performed that night, Dumbo climbed again to the top of the tall tower. He bravely held his magic feather and jumped off. Suddenly, it slipped from his trunk. Dumbo was falling fast. Timothy shouted that the feather wasn't really magic — Dumbo could fly all by himself!

At the last second, Dumbo flapped his ears. The crowd cheered. The people had never seen anything like the flying elephant with the amazing, enormous ears. Dumbo was a star.

Finding Nemo

Adapted by Michael Fertig
Illustrated by The Disney Storybook Artists

It was Nemo's first day of school and he was eager to impress the other kids in his class. They were daring each other to swim away from the dreaded drop-off and touch the bottom of a boat that was floating nearby. Nemo fearlessly swam to the boat. Nemo's father, Marlin, arrived on the scene. He was angry with Nemo for swimming so far away from the rest of his class. Marlin yelled at him in front of everyone. Nemo was embarassed. He was upset with his father for yelling at him.

Without thinking, Nemo yelled back at his father.

"I hate you," he said.

Nemo didn't really mean it, but before he could take it back, a scuba diver swam up right behind Nemo and captured him.

Marlin watched the whole thing and was horrified. The diver swam to the surface, hopped back into his boat with Nemo, and sped off. Marlin swam after the boat, but it was no use. The motorboat was just too fast.

Marlin frantically searched for someone who had seen which direction the boat was heading. He was beside himself and didn't know what to do. Marlin needed help.

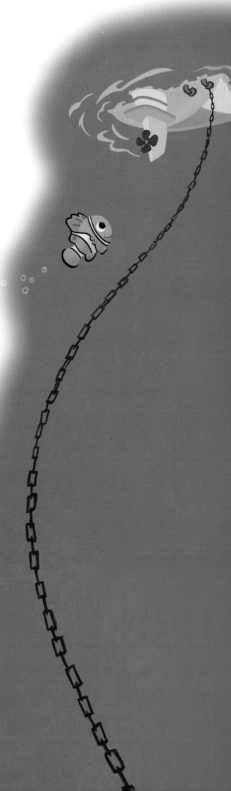

A regal blue tang fish by the name of Dory offered to help. However, Dory had a very short-term memory and almost immediately forgot that she was supposed to be helping Marlin. In fact, she thought that Marlin was chasing her.

Dory darted this way and that through the ocean water, trying to get away from her pursuer. Finally, Marlin was able to get Dory to stop. He explained to her why he was chasing her and she giggled at her own silliness. Then the duo set off to find Nemo and had all sorts of adventures. They were chased by sharks and stung by jellyfish, but they did find the address of the diver who took Nemo: 42 Wallaby Way, Sydney.

Meanwhile, Nemo found himself in the fish tank of a dentist, Dr. Sherman. Nemo learned that he was to be a present for Dr. Sherman's niece Darla. The other fish in the tank told Nemo that Darla was not very nice to her pet fish.

Just then, Nigel the pelican flew in the window with news of Marlin's adventures. He was on a quest to find Nemo!

Back in the ocean, Marlin and Dory continued their search for Nemo. They had just parted ways from a group of helpful sea turtles when the duo realized that they were lost. To make matters worse, a big whale scooped them right into his mouth. Marlin and Dory thought they were goners.

Much to their surprise, they found themselves soaring in a fountain of water above the surface of the ocean. The whale had pushed them out of his blowhole just off the coast of Sydney. Dory smiled at Marlin as they hung in the air.

They knew they were close, but they weren't out of trouble yet. The pair managed to find themselves surrounded by scores of hungry sea gulls. They were moments away from being breakfast for the birds when Nigel spotted the fish and rescued them, scooping them into his mouth.

Back in the dentist's office, Nemo was about to be given to Darla as a birthday gift. In an attempt to get flushed down the toilet — all pipes lead to the ocean — Nemo played dead.

As Nemo was floating upside down, Nigel had flown in the window of Dr. Sherman's office. Marlin spotted Nemo and thought he was dead. Nigel and Dory thought the same. Nigel flew away, offered his apologies, and deposited the two fish back into the ocean.

Back in the office, with the help of the other fish, Nemo was able to escape into one of Dr. Sherman's sinks and slip down the drain. He swam through the pipes until he popped out of a valve. Nemo found himself back in the ocean!

Thinking his son was gone, Marlin parted ways with Dory. As she swam away, Dory met Nemo right after he emerged from the pipe. After needing a moment to remember why it was important to find him, she led Nemo to Marlin. Marlin could not believe his eyes. Nemo was alive! The father and son hugged. They were thrilled to be back together again.

"Love ya, Dad," said Nemo as he hugged his father.

"I love you, too," said Marlin back to his son.

The Emperor's New Groove

Adapted by Gayla Amaral

Illustrated by the Disney Storybook Artists

Long ago, there lived a very selfish emperor named Kuzco. To celebrate his birthday, he decided to give himself a special gift—a summer vacation home in the best spot high on a hilltop. He would call it Kuzcotopia! After all, Kuzco was completely spoiled and lived in a perfect world where his every whim was met. Unfortunately, building his summer home meant destroying the village of the peasants who lived on the hilltop.

When one of the peasants, Pacha, was summoned to the palace, he discovered that Kuzco planned to destroy the village where Pacha's family had lived for generations. Because he was as generous and kind as Kuzco was selfish and mean, the peasant could hardly believe his ears!

"But where will we live?" wondered Pacha.
"Don't know! Don't care!" replied the emperor.

Kuzco's next item of business was to fire his evil and scary advisor, Yzma. The outraged Yzma hatched a sinister plan. A few drops of poison at dinner, and Kuzco would be dead before dessert! No sooner had Kuzco swallowed the poison than he was—dead? Not quite! Instead, he was a llama!

Furious, Yzma demanded that Kronk, her muscle-bound assistant, finish the job. But the blundering Kronk failed, and the llama emperor landed in the cart of the dismayed Pacha. Pacha agreed to take the emperor back to the palace, but only if Kuzco promised not to destroy the village.

"I don't make deals with peasants!" responded Kuzco, walking into the jungle. But Pacha believed there was goodness in everyone, even Kuzco. Pacha ran after the emperor and gave him another chance.
Kuzco finally promised ...
but it was all a lie.

Meanwhile at the castle, the wicked Yzma discovered that Kuzco was still alive, and set out with Kronk to find him. Fortunately, Kronk's days as a Junior Chipmunk led him into conversation with Bucky the squirrel. Squeakity squeaky! Bucky had seen the talking llama! A wild jungle chase began, ending at the palace where Pacha and the emperor searched Yzma's secret lab for the vial of potion that would turn Kuzco back into a human. Where could it be?

"Looking for this?" asked a sinister voice. It was Yzma, holding the vial they so desperately needed.

In the midst of a mad scramble for the vial was the simple-minded Kronk, who found himself torn between helping Yzma or the emperor. But goodness won out — and the vials, including the one they needed, fell into the hands of Kuzco and Pacha . . . or so it seemed.

Suddenly, down swooped Yzma, grabbing the vial and leaving them with bottles of seemingly useless potion! In the struggle, the remaining vials changed Kuzco from a turtle to a bird to a whale. And one of the potions turned Yzma into a small gray kitten. Just as the emperor spied the last vial on one ledge, he saw Pacha hanging precariously from another ledge.

Forced to choose between helping his new friend or grabbing the potion, the emperor chose to help Pacha. And with help from Kronk, the kindly peasant was rescued and the emperor was once again a human, and a much nicer one at that!

And they all lived happily ever after—with Kuzco's new summer home built on the hilltop next to Pacha's. And the emperor learned that a perfect world begins and ends with friends!

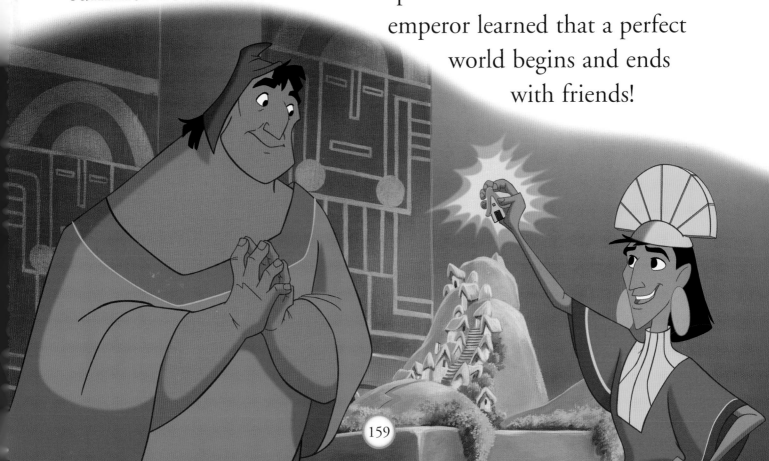